STATES OF MIND

I FEEL LOVED

BY STEPHANIE FINNE

BLUE OWL
BOOKS

TIPS FOR CAREGIVERS

Social and emotional learning (SEL) helps children manage emotions, create and achieve goals, maintain relationships, learn how to feel empathy, and make good decisions. The SEL approach will help children establish positive habits in communication, cooperation, and decision-making. By incorporating SEL in early reading, children will be better equipped to build confidence and foster positive peer networks.

BEFORE READING

Talk to the reader about love. Explain that love is a feeling of affection and respect.

Discuss: How does love feel to you? What actions and words make you feel loved? How do you show love to others?

AFTER READING

Talk to the reader about self-esteem and empathy. Explain that these help increase self-love.

Discuss: How can you increase your love for yourself? What are some things you can do to spread empathy?

SEL GOAL

Some students may struggle with relationship skills. They may need to be encouraged to think of how others think and feel. Help them identify what makes them feel loved. Then help them think about how others may want to be shown love.

TABLE OF CONTENTS

CHAPTER 1
Feeling Love 4

CHAPTER 2
Love Yourself 10

CHAPTER 3
Spreading Love 16

GOALS AND TOOLS
Grow with Goals 22
Try This! 22
Glossary 23
To Learn More 23
Index 24

FEELING LOVE

Have you felt love? Maybe you feel this when your pet wants to snuggle. Love makes us feel warm and happy. It can make us feel safe and protected. It can also make us feel proud and **confident**. These are all positive feelings and **emotions**!

Love is having a strong **affection** for someone or something. It can be based on trust, respect, kindness, or similar interests. You can love many things. And love can come from many people.

Love can be said with words. We tell those we love and trust, "I love you!" It can also be shown with actions. Craig shows his dad love with a hug.

LEVELS OF CLOSENESS

We feel closer to some people because we know they are safe and love us back. These people are OK to give hugs to. Other ways to show love and respect include high fives or handshakes.

Some people show love by doing nice things for others. Other people feel love when they spend **quality time** together. What makes you feel loved?

CHAPTER 2

LOVE YOURSELF

It feels good when someone loves you. It is also important to love yourself. Loving yourself gives you confidence to trust in yourself and try new things. It also helps you show love to others.

Things I'm good at:
I'm good at including others.
I'm good at saying thank you.
I'm good at helping at home.
I'm good at math.

There are many ways to find love for yourself. Make a list of your strengths and positive **traits**. Include things like being kind, being honest, and showing respect. Acknowledging these strengths and traits will help you build confidence and **self-love**.

Respecting your body is part
of self-love. Treat it well. How?
Eat healthy foods. Drink water.
Get plenty of sleep and exercise,
too. When you treat your body
well, you show it love and respect.

Love yourself by working hard. What does this mean? Push yourself to reach your **goals**. Believe in yourself. **Setbacks** happen. Tell yourself you can do it! This will help you build confidence. When you feel confident, you feel proud of yourself. This helps you love yourself!

TALK NICELY TO YOURSELF

It can be easy to feel bad about yourself. When that happens, talk to yourself like you talk to friends when they feel bad. Use positive **affirmations**. Say to yourself, "I am cared for," "I believe in myself," and "I am special!"

CHAPTER 3

SPREADING LOVE

You can help others feel love! How? Show respect and kindness. Include others, and take turns. Share something you have with someone else.

Let others know their strengths. Tell your friends and family members when they do a good job. Apologize when you haven't shown love. Learn how to forgive others.

Another way to spread love to yourself and others is to practice **gratitude**. Stop and think about what you are thankful for. You may be grateful for warm pajamas or a sunny day.

You can also show gratitude to others. Say thank you. Tell your parents you **appreciate** what they do for you.

RESPECT OTHERS

Love can look different to different people. For example, you may like hugs, but your friend doesn't. Show love by respecting others' wishes.

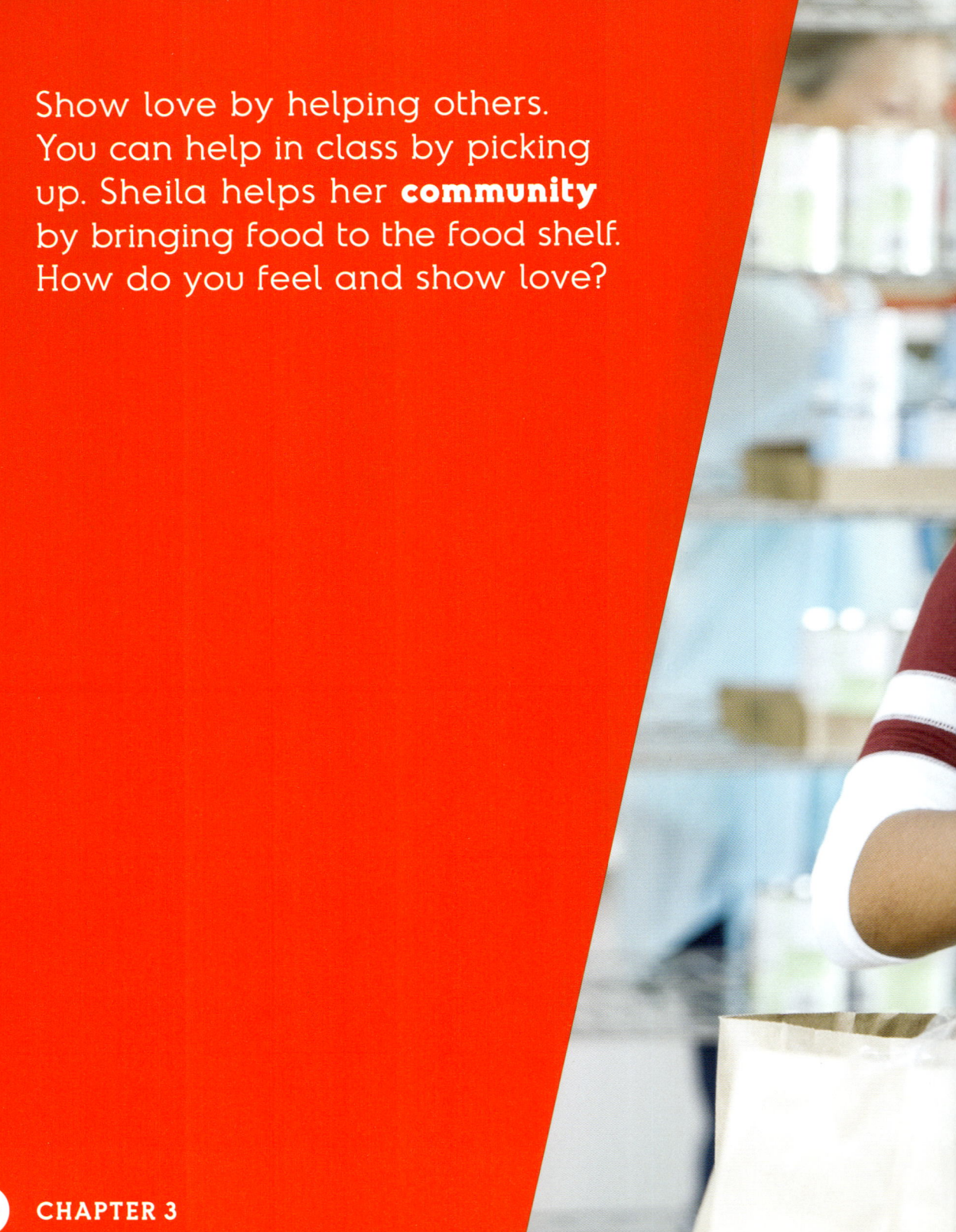

Show love by helping others. You can help in class by picking up. Sheila helps her **community** by bringing food to the food shelf. How do you feel and show love?

GOALS AND TOOLS

GROW WITH GOALS

Love can look different to different people. Part of showing love is respecting others' wishes and showing kindness. Try these things to build loving relationships.

Goal: Identify what makes you feel loved. Is it being safe? Is it when you feel cared for? Make a list of things that make you feel loved.

Goal: Talk to a friend about what love means to him or her. Ask what makes him or her feel loved. Pay attention to your friend's answers.

Goal: Spread kindness. This could be holding a door for someone or volunteering. It can even be as simple as smiling at someone. Spreading kindness is spreading love.

TRY THIS!

Start a gratitude journal. Each day, think about something you are thankful for. Write it down or draw it in the journal, even if it seems small. Reread your entries each week. How does it make you feel?

GLOSSARY

affection
Love for someone or something familiar to you.

affirmations
Things we repeatedly say to ourselves out loud or in our thoughts.

appreciate
To enjoy or value somebody or something.

community
A group of people who all have something in common.

confident
Self-assured and having a strong belief in your own abilities.

emotions
Feelings, such as happiness, sadness, or anger.

goals
Things you aim to do.

gratitude
A feeling of being grateful or thankful.

quality time
Time spent giving another person one's undivided attention.

self-love
Regard for one's own well-being and happiness.

setbacks
Problems that delay you or keep you from making progress.

traits
Qualities or characteristics that make people different from each other.

TO LEARN MORE

FACT SURFER

Finding more information is as easy as 1, 2, 3.

1. Go to www.factsurfer.com

2. Enter "**Ifeelloved**" into the search box.

3. Choose your cover to see a list of websites.

INDEX

affection 5

affirmations 14

apologize 17

appreciate 19

body 13

community 20

confident 4, 10, 11, 14

exercise 13

forgive 17

goals 14

handshakes 7

happy 4

high fives 7

hug 7, 19

kindness 5, 11, 16

proud 4, 14

quality time 8

respect 5, 7, 11, 13, 16, 19

safe 4, 7

self-love 11, 13

share 16

sleep 13

traits 11

trust 5, 7, 10

warm 4, 19

words 7

Blue Owl Books are published by Jump!, 5357 Penn Avenue South, Minneapolis, MN 55419, www.jumplibrary.com

Copyright © 2021 Jump! International copyright reserved in all countries. No part of this book may be reproduced in any form without written permission from the publisher.

Library of Congress Cataloging-in-Publication Data

Names: Finne, Stephanie, author.
Title: I feel loved / by Stephanie Finne.
Description: Minneapolis, MN: Jump!, [2021] | Series: States of mind
Audience: Ages 7–10 | Audience: Grades 2–3
Identifiers: LCCN 2019052385 (print)
LCCN 2019052386 (ebook)
ISBN 9781645274049 (library binding)
ISBN 9781645274056 (paperback)
ISBN 9781645274063 (ebook)
Subjects: LCSH: Love in children—Juvenile literature.
Classification: LCC BF723.L69 F56 2021 (print)
LCC BF723.L69 (ebook) | DDC 155.4/1241—dc23
LC record available at https://lccn.loc.gov/2019052385
LC ebook record available at https://lccn.loc.gov/2019052386

Editor: Jenna Gleisner
Designer: Molly Ballanger

Photo Credits: Roman Samborskyi/Shutterstock, cover; Krakenimages.com/Shutterstock, 1; Ronnachai Palas/Shutterstock, 3; Phichat Phruksarojanakun/Shutterstock, 4; LumiNola/iStock, 5; SDI Productions/iStock, 6–7, 20–21; FG Trade/iStock, 8–9; nakaridore/Shutterstock, 10; TrinsetWRP/Shutterstock, 11; SolStock/iStock, 12–13; antoniodiaz/Shutterstock, 14–15; Birgid Allig/Corbis/Getty, 16; Vereshchagin Dmitry/Shutterstock, 17 (background); Image_Source_/iStock, 17 (foreground); RgStudio/iStock, 18–19.

Printed in the United States of America at Corporate Graphics in North Mankato, Minnesota.